©P.F.V.& CO.

MOTHER GOOSE

The Classic Volland Edition

MOTHER GOOSE

The Classic Volland Edition

Rearranged and edited in this form by
EULALIE OSGOOD GROVER

Illustrated by
FREDERICK RICHARDSON

RAND McNALLY & COMPANY
CHICAGO · NEW YORK · SAN FRANCISCO

Dedicated by the
Compiler *and* Artist
to
VIRGINIA *and* DORIS
and their mother

Library of Congress Cataloging in Publication Data
Mother Goose.
    Mother Goose.
  Reprint of the edition published by Hubbard Press,
Northbrook, Illinois.
  Includes index.
Summary: A collection of illustrated Mother Goose
rhymes such as Old Mother Hubbard and Goosey, goosey,
gander.
    1. Nursery rhymes.   (1. Nursery rhymes)   I. Grover,
Eulalie Osgood, 1873–   II. Richardson, Frederick,
1862–1937.   III. Title.
PZ8.3.M85Groll   398.8   76–16156
ISBN 0–528–88559–6
(previously ISBN 0–8331–0016–5)

AN INTRODUCTION

by YOLANDA D. FEDERICI
Director of Children's Books
Chicago Public Library

Mother Goose and the rhymes attributed to her are acknowledged favorites with children. Young children, even the littlest ones, show preferences in their choice of the sounds, words and books they want to hear read aloud. Before their hands can hold books, babies show an interest in the rhythmic lilt of Mother Goose rhymes. A three-month-old baby, for example, will listen with a wondering intentness to "Little Bo-peep has lost her sheep." And "Bye, Baby Bunting," or "Hush-a-Bye, Baby," have a soothing rhythm that will lull a child to sleep. The many finger games and plays that identify parts of the body, like "This little pig went to market," will bring many moments of delight. When the child has some control of his arms and hands, he will take part in, "Pat a cake, pat a cake," and many of the other action rhymes. Later, the picture book itself will attract the children, and they will point to the colorful illustrations that accompany their favorite rhymes and demand that those be read.

As children grow, they learn the riddles and the ABC and counting rhymes. Then they want the longer ballads read aloud. There is actually something for everyone in Mother Goose. Even scholarly adults are intrigued by her possible origin, by the hidden meaning in the simple verses, and even which particular historical characters are being lampooned in them. Parents share with their children their own pleasant memories of hours of fun as children with such rhymes as "Hickery, Dickery, Dock," "Bah, Bah, black sheep," and all the other old friends in Mother Goose. Few books have the quality of appeal that lasts from one generation to another.

The longevity of this old lady and her offerings is probably due to the folk quality that is inherent in her origin as much as the lively nonsense, good commonsense, and variety in the verses. Some of the rhymes can be traced to popular ballads, folk songs and games, political satire, ancient proverbs, cries of street vendors, real or legendary events. These were known long before they were designated as Mother Goose rhymes. In fact, until the eighteenth century Mother Goose did not have a name in print in English literature.

Her name may have come from Charlemagne's mother who was known as Queen Goosefoot. *Mère l'Oye,* or Mother Goose, was well known in

France for centuries as the supposed originator of any fabulous tale, particularly those for children.

Additions from old sources keep on increasing the number of pieces attributed to Mother Goose. These are taken from old proverbs, riddles, charms, and tongue-twisters. When adequate research is not done, familiar poems for children, whose authorship is declared anonymous, are frequently included. For example, "Twinkle, Twinkle Little Star" was written by Jane Taylor. Sara J. Hale wrote "Mary Had a Little Lamb," and Eliza Lee Follen wrote "The Three Little Kittens."

In every generation, distinguished authors and artists have felt the lure of doing their own Mother Goose collection. There is something about this folk character and her rhymes that stimulates imaginative people who remember her charm for young children, and who want to add their own interpretation. Mother Goose has worn many different costumes but those that seem to suit her best are the ones currently worn as everyday clothing during the eighteenth century when she first acquired her name in print.

Her perennial attraction for children is the variety of interesting characters that troop through the pages of her books, and not all of the characters are good. "Little Boy Blue," for example, is asleep on the job. "Little Polly Flinders" is a careless little girl. And Simple Simon did his best to get something for nothing from the pieman. But Mother Goose is full of happy, busy children who are independent and ingenious. Another attraction is the natural contact that the child-characters have with the great grown-up world. The rhymes tell about festivals, vocations, courtship, marriage, and death. There are many adult characters in adult situations, like "Jack Sprat could eat no fat," "There was a crooked man," "Old woman, old woman, shall we go a-shearing?" "A Farmer went trotting upon his gray mare," and many others.

Friendly animals are everywhere, with cats and mice as special favorites, as in "I like little pussy, her coat is so warm," and "Hickery, Dickery, Dock/ The mouse ran up the clock." Other rhymes are humorous and full of fantasy, such as "High diddle diddle/The cat and the fiddle" and "Three wise men of Gotham/Went to sea in a bowl." For older children, there is a more mature humor as in "The man in the wilderness/Asked me/How many strawberries/Grew in the sea." Action-filled and quickly resolved plots also charm the young and the older children: "The Queen of hearts/She made some tarts," "Sing a song of sixpence," "Old King Cole," and so on. Then there are the riddles which seem at first glance incomprehensible yet always fascinate the young.

Here is the wealth of Mother Goose presented for the delight of children and adults of all ages. She is a very old lady who remains youthful and vigorous; and remarkably she is able to charm every new generation.

A FOREWORD

Children, as well as their interested parents, will eagerly welcome this beautiful edition of the one great nursery classic, just as a worthy edition of Shakespeare is welcomed by discriminating adult readers.

But some may ask what there is in these simple melodies, attributed to Mother Goose, which gives them so secure and beloved a place in the home, the school and the public library. Is it the humor, the action, the rhythm, or the mystery of the theme which appeals so strongly to critical little minds in each generation of childhood, and even to adult minds so fortunate as to have retained some of the refreshing naiveté of early years?

It is useless to try to explain the charm of these nonsense melodies. The children themselves do not know why they love them. No mother can tell us the magic of the spell which seems to be cast over her restless baby as she croons to it a Mother Goose lullaby. No primary teacher quite understands why the mere repetition or singing of a Mother Goose jingle will transform her listless, inattentive class into one all eagerness and attention. But mother and teacher agree that the best of these verses have an even more potent influence than that of innocently diverting and entertaining the child. The healthy moral, so subtly suggested in many of the rhymes, is unconsciously absorbed by the child's receptive mind, helping him to make his own distinction between right and wrong, bravery and cowardice, generosity and selfishness.

From a literary standpoint, also, these rhymes have proved of real value in creating a taste for the truly musical in poetry and song. They train the ear and stir the imagination of the child as no other verses do. Many famous poets and writers trace their first inspiration, and love for things literary, back to the nursery songs and fairy tales of their childhood.

Teachers well know that children who have reveled in these rhymes and stories, at the time of their strongest appeal, step naturally and appreciatively into the great fields of good literature which are beyond.

Knowing these things to be true, we do not hesitate to place this venerable classic on the shelf beside our Shakespeare, and to send our children there for delight and inspiration. They will understand Shakespeare the better for having known and loved Mother Goose.

But what about the personality of this classic writer? Was she really Mistress Elizabeth Goose who is said to have lived in Boston about two hundred years ago, and who crooned her nonsense jingles to a large and happy family of grandchildren? We are told that their father, Thomas Fleet, who was a printer by trade, thought to turn an honesty penny with his mother-in-law's popular verses, so he published them in a small volume under the title of "Songs for the Nursery: or, Mother Goose's Melodies." A goose with a very long neck and a wide-open mouth flew across the title page, at least so the story goes. But we have to believe that it is only a story, for no copy of the book can be found, and nothing but tradition identifies Elizabeth Goose, the Boston grandmother, with the famous rhymester.

We might feel sorry to be obliged to discredit this picturesque story of Mother Goose, if her real history were not even more mysterious. We know very little about the beloved patron of childhood, but what we do know is as follows:

Mother Goose is most certainly of respectable French origin, for in 1697 a distinguished French writer, Charles Perrault, published in Paris a little book of familiar stories called "Contes de ma Mère l'Oye," or "Tales of My Mother Goose." Her identity, however, he leaves a mystery, except that in the frontispiece of his book is pictured an old woman by her fireside telling stories to an eager little family group.

This volume contained the only prose tales that have ever been credited to Mother Goose, and they are still among the most popular

stories in nursery or school room. The titles are as follows: "Little Red Riding Hood;" "The Sisters Who Dropped From Their Mouths Diamonds and Toads;" "Bluebeard;" "The Sleeping Beauty;" "Puss in Boots;" "Cinderella;" "Riquet With the Tuft;" and "Tom Thumb."

It is through her verses, however, that Mother Goose has won her well-deserved fame. The first collection under her name was published in London about 1765 by John Newbery. It may be, if Oliver Goldsmith were living, he could tell us more about the origin of these verses than we are now ever likely to know. It is more than probable that he himself edited the little volume for John Newbery, and that he wrote the clever preface, "By a very Great Writer of very Little Books," as well as the quaint moral which supplements each rhyme.

About twenty-five years later this book was reprinted in our country by Isaiah Thomas of Worcester, Massachusetts. Several copies of this edition are preserved, one of which has been photographed and reproduced in facsimile by W. H. Whitmore of Boston. Other publishers also reprinted the English edition, one being done for John Newbery's grandson, Francis Power, in 1791.

In 1810 another collection of melodies appeared under the title of "Gammer Gurton's Garland." It was quite evidently a rival of Mother Goose, though it contained nearly all of her verses, besides many far less interesting ones gathered from other sources.

Gammer Gurton's popularity, however, was short, and Mother Goose was revived about 1825 by a Boston firm, Munroe and Francis. Since that time her fame has never waned. In spite of the present multiplicity of beautiful books for children, they are constantly exhausting large editions of the one universally beloved book of melodies. Some of these volumes have been collected and edited by men of the highest literary judgment and ability, such as Goldsmith (with hardly a doubt), Ritson, Halliwell, Andrew Lang, Charles Eliot Norton, Charles Welsh and Edward Everett Hale. Certainly there is not another collection of juvenile literature which can boast such a list of scholarly editors. The deepest gratitude is due them for their careful and discriminating effort to pre-

serve for the children of future generations this rich heritage of nursery melodies.

Many less discriminating editors, however, have ruthlessly mutilated and adapted many of the rhymes to suit their fancy, thinking, possibly, that as Mother Goose is only a title, the verses attributed to her belong to the general public to use as it sees fit. On the contrary, Mother Goose's melodies belong to the children, and no addition or change should be made except by those who are in such close sympathy with the child-heart that they may act with the child's authority.

This present edition of "Mother Goose" preserves the best of the verses which became so popular in England and America as to first demand their publication. It is the only truly classic edition that has been published in modern times. The two authorities which have been followed are the edition published for John Newbery's grandson in London in 1791, and probably edited by Oliver Goldsmith, and the edition published in Boston in 1833 by Munroe and Francis, called "The Only True Mother Goose Melodies." It is from this copy that the following quaint introduction by "Ma'am Goose" is quoted.

Not all the favorites among the nursery rhymes are here, only those that first helped to make the fame of the fictitious but no less worthy patron of childhood. May her fame and her melodies be lovingly preserved to give joy and inspiration to many future generations of little children.

EULALIE OSGOOD GROVER

Hear What Ma'am Goose Says!

My dear little Blossoms, there are now in this world, and always will be, a great many grannies besides myself, both in petticoats and pantaloons, some a deal younger, to be sure, but all monstrous wise and of my own family name. These old women, who never had chick or child of their own, but who always know how to bring up other people's children, will tell you with long faces that my enchanting, quieting, soothing volume, my all-sufficient anodyne for cross, peevish, won't-be-comforted little bairns, ought be laid aside for more learned books, such as *they* could select and publish. Fudge! I tell you that all their batterings can't deface my beauties, nor their wise pratings equal my wiser prattlings; and all imitators of my refreshing songs might as well write another Billy Shakespeare as another Mother Goose—we two great poets were born together, and shall go out of the world together.

No, no, my melodies will never die,
While nurses sing, or babies cry.

THE VOLLAND CREED

It is the Volland ideal that books for children should contain nothing to cause fright, suggest fear, glorify mischief, extenuate malice or condone cruelty. That is why they are called "books good for children"

From "The Only True Mother Goose Melodies
Published by Munroe & Francis, Boston, 1833

OLD MOTHER GOOSE

Old Mother Goose, when
  She wanted to wander,
Would ride through the air
  On a very fine gander.

Mother Goose had a house,
  'Twas built in a wood,
An owl at the door
  For a porter stood.

She had a son Jack,
  A plain-looking lad,
He was not very good,
  Nor yet very bad.

She sent him to market,
  A live goose he bought:
"Here! mother," says he,
  "It will not go for nought."

Jack's goose and her gander
  Grew very fond;
They'd both eat together,
  Or swim in one pond.

Jack found one morning,
  As I have been told,
His goose had laid him
  An egg of pure gold.

Jack rode to his mother,
  The news for to tell.
She called him a good boy,
  And said it was well.

And Old Mother Goose
  The goose saddled soon,
And mounting its back,
  Flew up to the moon.

Old Mother Goose, when
  She wanted to wander,
Would ride through the air
  On a very fine gander.

Cock-a-doodle-doo,
My dame has lost her shoe:
My master's lost his fiddlestick,
And knows not what to do.

14

Peter, Peter, pumpkin eater,
Had a wife and couldn't keep her;
He put her in a pumpkin shell,
And then he kept her very well.

Peter, Peter, pumpkin eater,
Had another, and didn't love her;
Peter learned to read and spell,
And then he loved her very well.

I had a little hobby-horse,
And it was dapple gray;
Its head was made of pea-straw,
Its tail was made of hay.
I sold it to an old woman
For a copper groat;
And I'll not sing my song again
Without another coat.

Monday's bairn is fair of face,
Tuesday's bairn is full of grace,
Wednesday's bairn is full of woe,
Thursday's bairn has far to go,
Friday's bairn is loving and giving,
Saturday's bairn works hard for its
    living;
But the bairn that is born on the
    Sabbath day
Is bonny and blithe and good and
    gay.

Three young rats with black felt
    hats,
Three young ducks with white
    straw flats,
Three young dogs with curling
    tails,
Three young cats with demi-veils,
Went out to walk with three
    young pigs
In satin vests and sorrel wigs;
But suddenly it chanced to rain
And so they all went home again.

"Billy, Billy, come and play,
While the sun shines bright as day."

"Yes, my Polly, so I will,
For I love to please you still."

"Billy, Billy, have you seen
Sam and Betsy on the green?"

"Yes, my Poll, I saw them pass,
Skipping o'er the new-mown grass."

"Billy, Billy, come along,
And I will sing a pretty song."

Hie to the market, Jenny come trot,
Spilt all her buttermilk, every drop,
Every drop and every dram,
Jenny came home with an
    empty can.

Shoe the colt,
Shoe the colt,
Shoe the wild mare;
Here a nail,
There a nail,
Colt must go bare.

If all the world were apple pie,
And all the sea were ink,
And all the trees were bread and
    cheese,
What should we have to drink?

Lady-bird, Lady-bird,
Fly away home,
Your house is on fire,
Your children will burn.

One misty, moisty morning,
  When cloudy was the weather,
I chanced to meet an old man clothed all in leather.
He began to compliment, and I began to grin,
  How do you do, and how do you do?
  And how do you do again?

I like little pussy, her coat is so warm,
And if I don't hurt her she'll do me no harm;
So I'll not pull her tail, nor drive her away,
But pussy and I very gently will play.

Little Bo-peep has lost her sheep,
And can't tell where to find them;
Leave them alone, and they'll come home,
And bring their tails behind them.

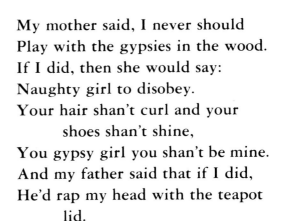

Mary had a little lamb
    With fleece as white as snow.
And everywhere that Mary went
    The lamb was sure to go.

It followed her to school one day—
    That was against the rule.
It made the children laugh and
      play
    To see a lamb at school.

And so the teacher turned it out,
    But still it lingered near,
And waited patiently about
    Till Mary did appear.

"Why does the lamb love Mary so?"
    The eager children cry.
"Why, Mary loves the lamb, you
      know!"
    The teacher did reply.

Birds of a feather flock together,
And so will pigs and swine;
Rats and mice have their choice,
And so will I have mine.

    Go to bed first,
    A golden purse;
    Go to bed second,
    A golden pheasant;
    Go to bed third,
    A golden bird.

My mother said, I never should
Play with the gypsies in the wood.
If I did, then she would say:
Naughty girl to disobey.
Your hair shan't curl and your
    shoes shan't shine,
You gypsy girl you shan't be mine.
And my father said that if I did,
He'd rap my head with the teapot
    lid.

My mother said that I never should
Play with the gypsies in the wood.
The wood was dark, the grass was
    green;
By came Sally with a tambourine.
I went to sea—no ship to get
    across;
I paid ten shillings for a blind
    white horse.
I upped on his back and was off
    in a crack,
Sally tell my mother I shall never
    come back.

There's a neat little clock,—
In the schoolroom it stands,—
And it points to the time
With its two little hands.

And may we, like the clock,
Keep a face clean and bright,
With hands ever ready
To do what is right.

Little Nanny Etticoat
In a white petticoat,
　　And a red nose;
The longer she stands
　　The shorter she grows.

Jack, be nimble; Jack, be quick;
Jack, jump over the candlestick.

Who killed Cock Robin?
"I," said the sparrow,
"With my little bow and arrow,
I killed Cock Robin."

Who saw him die?
"I," said the fly,
"With my little eye,
I saw him die."

Who caught his blood?
"I," said the fish,
"With my little dish,
I caught his blood."

Who'll make his shroud?
"I," said the beetle,
"With my thread and needle.
I'll make his shroud."

Who'll carry the torch?
"I," said the linnet,
"I'll come in a minute,
I'll carry the torch."

Who'll be the clerk?
"I," said the lark,
"If it's not in the dark,
I'll be the clerk."

Who'll dig his grave?
"I," said the owl,
"With my spade and trowel
I'll dig his grave."

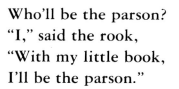

Who'll be the parson?
"I," said the rook,
"With my little book,
I'll be the parson."

Who'll be chief mourner?
"I," said the dove,
"I mourn for my love,
I'll be chief mourner."

Who'll sing a psalm?
"I," said the thrush,
"As I sit in a bush.
I'll sing a psalm."

Who'll carry the coffin?
"I," said the kite,
"If it's not in the night,
I'll carry the coffin."

Who'll toll the bell?
"I," said the bull,
"Because I can pull,
I'll toll the bell."

All the birds of the air
Fell sighing and sobbing,
When they heard the bell toll
For poor Cock Robin.

Rain, rain, go away,
Come again another day;
Little Johnny wants to play.

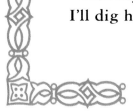

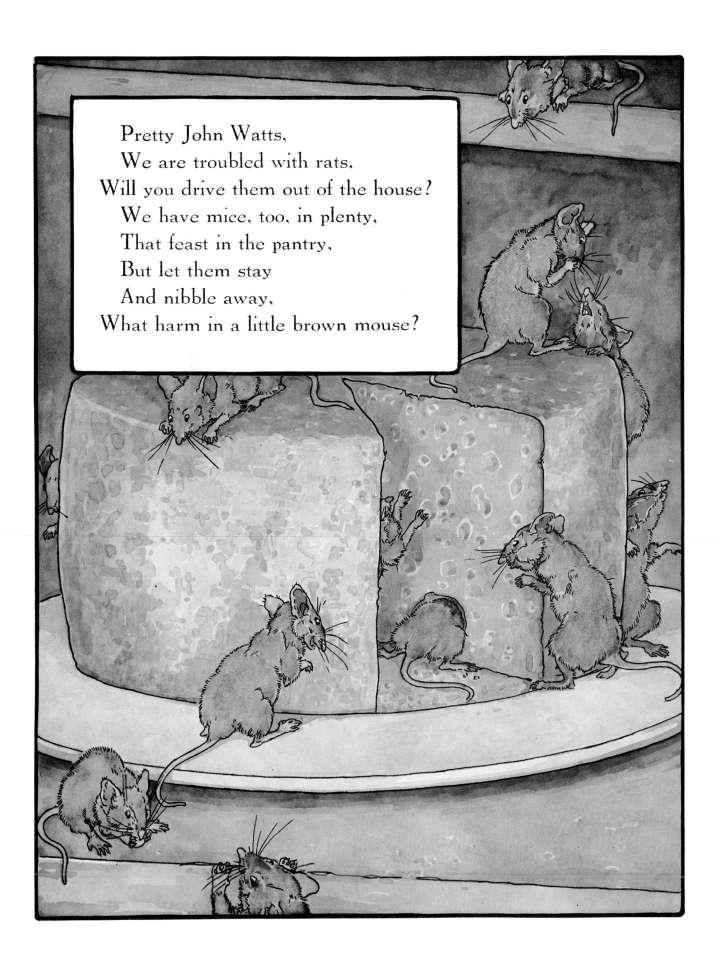

Pretty John Watts,
We are troubled with rats,
Will you drive them out of the house?
We have mice, too, in plenty,
That feast in the pantry,
But let them stay
And nibble away,
What harm in a little brown mouse?

I'll tell you a story
About Mary Morey,
And now my story's begun.
I'll tell you another
About her brother,
And now my story's done.

Hush-a-bye, Baby, upon the tree top,
When the wind blows the cradle will rock;
When the bough breaks the cradle will fall,
Down tumbles cradle and Baby and all.

Ride away, ride away,
 Johnny shall ride,
And he shall have pussy-cat
 Tied to one side;
And he shall have little dog
 Tied to the other,
And Johnny shall ride
 To see his grandmother.

Little Jenny Wren fell sick,
Upon a time;
In came Robin Redbreast
And brought her cake and wine.

"Eat well of my cake, Jenny,
Drink well of my wine."
"Thank you, Robin, kindly,
You shall be mine."

Jenny she got well,
And stood upon her feet,
And told Robin plainly
She loved him not a bit.

Robin being angry,
Hopped upon a twig,
Saying, "Out upon you! Fie upon
    you!
Bold-faced jig!"

Dance, little baby, dance up high!
Never mind, baby, mother is by.
Crow and caper, caper and crow,
There, little Baby, there you go!

Up to the ceiling, down to the
    ground,
Backwards and forwards, round
    and round;
Dance, little baby and mother will
    sing,
With the merry coral, ding, ding,
    ding!

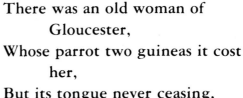

There was an old woman of
    Gloucester,
Whose parrot two guineas it cost
    her,
But its tongue never ceasing,
Was vastly displeasing
To the talkative woman of
    Gloucester.

I am a pretty wench,
And I come a great way
    hence,
And sweethearts I can get
    none:
But every dirty sow
Can get sweethearts enough,
And I pretty wench can get
    none.

What are little boys made of,
    made of?
What are little boys made of?
Snaps and snails and puppy dogs
    tails;
And that's what little boys are
    made of, made of.

What are little girls made of,
    made of?
What are little girls made of?
Sugar and spice and all that's nice;
And that's what little girls are
    made of, made of.

Dickery, dickery, dock,
The mouse ran up the clock;
The clock struck one,
The mouse ran down,
Dickery, dickery, dock.

A, B, C, D, E, F, G,
H, I, J, K, L, M, N, O, P,
Q, R, S, and T, U, V,
W, X, and Y and Z.
Now I've said my A, B, C,
Tell me what you think of me.

The little robin grieves
    When the snow is on the ground,
For the trees have no leaves,
    And no berries can be found.

The air is cold, the worms are hid;
    For robin here what can be done?
Let's strow around some crumbs of bread,
    And then he'll live till snow is gone.

Bobby Shaftoe's gone to sea,
Silver buckles on his knee;
He'll come back and marry me,
        Pretty Bobby Shaftoe.

Bobby Shaftoe's fat and fair,
Combing down his yellow hair,
He's my love forevermore,
        Pretty Bobby Shaftoe.

See-saw, sacradown,
Which is the way to London town?
One foot up, the other foot down,
That is the way to London town.

A cat came fiddling out of a barn,
With a pair of bagpipes under her
    arm;
She could sing nothing but fiddle-
    de-dee,
The mouse has married the
    bumble-bee;
Pipe, cat—dance, mouse—
We'll have a wedding at our good
    house.

Little Betty Blue
Lost her holiday shoe.
What will poor Betty do?
Why, give her another
To match the other,
And then she will walk in two.

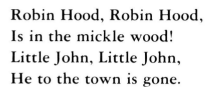

Robin Hood, Robin Hood,
Is in the mickle wood!
Little John, Little John,
He to the town is gone.

Robin Hood, Robin Hood,
Telling his beads,
All in the greenwood
Among the green weeds.

Little John, Little John,
If he comes no more,
Robin Hood, Robin Hood,
We shall fret full sore!

There was a lady loved a swine,
Honey, quoth she,
Pig-hog wilt thou be mine?
Hoogh, quoth he.

I'll build thee a silver sty,
Honey, quoth she,
And in it thou shalt lie.
Hoogh, quoth he.

Pinned with a silver pin,
Honey, quoth she,
That thou may go out and in.
Hoogh, quoth he.

Wilt thou have me now,
Honey? quoth she.
Speak or my heart will break.
Hoogh, quoth he.

Little Tommy Tittlemouse
Lived in a little house;
He caught fishes
In other men's ditches.

About the bush, Willie, about the bee-hive,
About the bush, Willie, I'll meet thee alive.

Bah, bah, black sheep,
  Have you any wool?
Yes, marry, have I,
  Three bags full;
One for my master,
  One for my dame,
But none for the little boy
  Who cries in the lane.

Hickety, pickety, my black hen,
She lays eggs for gentlemen:
Gentlemen come every day
To see what my black hen doth lay.

Three little kittens lost their
    mittens,
    And they began to cry,
    Oh! mother dear, we very
        much fear
    That we have lost our mittens.
Lost your mittens! You naughty
    kittens!
    Then you shall have no pie.
        Mee-ow, mee-ow, mee-ow.
    No, you shall have no pie.
        Mee-ow, mee-ow, mee-ow.

The three little kittens found their
    mittens,
    And they began to cry,
    Oh! mother dear, see here, see
        here,
    See, we have found our
        mittens.
Put on your mittens, you silly
    kittens,
    And you may have some pie.
        Purr-r, purr-r, purr-r,
    Oh! let us have the pie,
        Purr-r, purr-r, purr-r.

The three little kittens put on
    their mittens,
    And soon ate up the pie;
    Oh! mother dear, we greatly
        fear
    That we have soiled our
        mittens.

Soiled your mittens! you naughty
    kittens!
    Then they began to sigh,
        Mee-ow, mee-ow, mee-ow.
    Then they began to sigh,
        Mee-ow, mee-ow, mee-ow.

The three little kittens washed
    their mittens,
    And hung them out to dry;
    Oh! mother dear, do you not
        hear,
    That we have washed our
        mittens.
Washed your mittens! Oh! you're
    good kittens.
    But I smell a rat close by.
        Hush! hush! mee-ow.
        mee-ow.
    We smell a rat close by,
        Mee-ow, mee-ow, mee-ow.

Tweedle-dum and Tweedle-dee
Resolved to have a battle,
For Tweedle-dum said Tweedle-
    dee
Had spoiled his nice new rattle.
Just then flew by a monstrous
    crow,
As big as a tar barrel,
Which frightened both the
    heroes so,
They quite forgot their quarrel.

Willie boy, Willie boy,
  Where are you going?
O, let us go with you
  This sunshiny day.

I'm going to the meadow
  To see them a-mowing,
I'm going to help the girls
  Turn the new hay.

Three children sliding on the ice
   Upon a summer's day,
As it fell out, they all fell in,
   The rest they ran away.

Oh, had these children been at school,
   Or sliding on dry ground,
Ten thousand pounds to one penny
   They had not then been drowned.

Ye parents who have children dear,
   And ye, too, who have none,
If you would keep them safe abroad,
   Pray keep them safe at home.

Wee Willie Winkie runs through the town,
Upstairs and downstairs, in his nightgown;
Tapping at the window, crying at the lock:
"Are the babes in their beds, for it's now ten o'clock?

There was an old woman who lived in a shoe,
She had so many children she didn't know what to do.
She gave them some broth without any bread,
She whipped them all soundly and put them to bed.

Peter Piper picked a peck of
    pickled peppers;
A peck of pickled peppers Peter
    Piper picked.
If Peter Piper picked a peck of
    pickled peppers,
Where's the peck of pickled
    peppers
Peter Piper picked?

When I was a little girl,
About seven years old,
I hadn't got a petticoat,
To cover me from the cold.

So I went into Darlington,
That pretty little town,
And there I bought a petticoat,
A cloak, and a gown.

I went into the woods
And built me a kirk,
And all the birds of the air,
They helped me to work.

The hawk with his long claws
Pulled down the stone,
The dove with her rough bill
Brought me them home.

The parrot was the clergyman,
The peacock was the clerk,
The bullfinch played the organ,
We made merry work.

Here we go round the mulberry
    bush,
The mulberry bush, the mulberry
    bush,
Here we go round the mulberry
    bush.
On a cold and frosty morning.

This is the way we wash our
    hands,
Wash our hands, wash our hands,
This is the way we wash our
    hands,
On a cold and frosty morning.

This is the way we wash our
    clothes.
Wash our clothes, wash our
    clothes,
This is the way we wash our
    clothes,
On a cold and frosty morning.

This is the way we go to school,
Go to school, go to school,
This is the way we go to school,
On a cold and frosty morning.

This is the way we come out of
    school,
Come out of school, come out of
    school,
This is the way we come out of
    school,
On a cold and frosty morning.

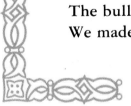

There was a man and he had naught,
 And robbers came to rob him;
He crept up to the chimney top,
 And then they thought they had him.
But he got down on the other side,
 And then they could not find him;
He ran fourteen miles in fifteen days,
 And never looked behind him.

There was an old man,
And he had a calf,
And that's half;
He took him out of the stall,
And put him on the wall,
And that's all.

Georgy Porgy, pudding and pie,
Kissed the girls and made them
    cry.
When the boys came out to play,
Georgy Porgy ran away.

"Where are you going to, my pretty
    maid?"
"I'm going a-milking, sir," she said.
"May I go with you, my pretty
    maid?"
"You're kindly welcome, sir," she
    said.
"What is your father, my pretty
    maid?"
"My father's a farmer, sir," she
    said.
"What is your fortune, my pretty
    maid?"
"My face is my fortune, sir," she
    said.
"Then I can't marry you, my pretty
    maid!"
"Nobody asked you, sir!" she said.

My Maid Mary she minds the
    dairy,
While I go a-hoeing and mowing
    each morn;
Gaily run the reel and the little
    spinning wheel.
While I am singing and mowing
    my corn.

Dear, dear! what can the matter be?
Two old women got up in an
    apple tree;
One came down, and the other
    stayed till Saturday.

If all the seas were one sea,
What a great sea that would be!
And if all the trees were one tree,
What a great tree that would be!
And if all the axes were one axe,
What a great axe that would be!
And if all the men were one man,
What a great man he would be!
And if the great man took the
    great axe,
And cut down the great tree,
And let it fall into the great sea,
What a splish splash that would be!

Thirty white horses upon a red
    hill,
Now they tramp, now they champ,
Now they stand still.

A wise old owl sat in an oak,
The more he heard the less he
    spoke;
The less he spoke the more he
    heard.
Why aren't we all like that wise
    old bird?

Bow, wow, wow!
Whose dog art thou?
Little Tom Tinker's dog,
Bow, wow, wow!

Pussy-Cat sits by the fire;
    How can she be fair?
In walks the little dog;
    Says: "Pussy, are you there?
How do you do, Mistress Pussy?
    Mistress Pussy, how d'ye do?"
"I thank you kindly, little dog,
    I fare as well as you!"

Here am I, little jumping Joan,
When nobody's with me
    I'm always alone.

Jog on, jog on, the footpath way,
  And merrily jump the style,
    boys;
A merry heart goes all the day,
  Your sad one tires in a mile,
    boys.

There was an old woman had
    three sons,
Jerry and James and John,
Jerry was hanged, James was
    drowned,
John was lost and never was
    found;
And there was an end of her three
    sons,
Jerry and James and John!

Every lady in this land
Has twenty nails, upon each hand
Five, and twenty on hands and
    feet:
All this is true, without deceit.

Over the water, and over the sea,
And over the water to Charley,
I'll have none of your nasty beef,
Nor I'll have none of your barley;
But I'll have some of your very
    best flour
To make a white cake for my
    Charley.

Johnny shall have a new bonnet,
  And Johnny shall go to the
    fair,
And Johhny shall have a blue
    ribbon
  To tie up his bonny brown
    hair.
And why may not I love Johnny?
  And why may not Johnny love
    me?
And why may not I love Johnny,
  As well as another body?
And here's a leg for a stocking,
  And here's a leg for a shoe,
And here's a kiss for his daddy,
  And two for his mammy, I
    trow.
And why may not I love Johnny?
  And why may not Johnny love
    me?
And why may not I love Johnny,
  As well as another body?

There were once two cats of
    Kilkenny.
Each thought there was one cat
    too many;
So they fought and they fit,
And they scratched and they bit,
Till, excepting their nails,
And the tips of their tails,
Instead of two cats, there weren't
    any.

There was an old woman lived under the hill,
And if she's not gone she lives there still.
Baked apples she sold, and cranberry pies,
And she's the old woman that never told lies.

Simple Simon met a pieman
   Going to the fair;
Says Simple Simon to the pieman:
  "Pray let me taste your ware."

Says the pieman to Simple Simon:
  "Show me first your penny;"
Says Simple Simon to the pieman:
  "Indeed I have not any."

Sing a song of sixpence, a bag full of rye,
Four and twenty blackbirds baked in a pie;
When the pie was opened the birds began to sing,
And wasn't this a dainty dish to set before the king?
The king was in the parlor counting out his money;
The queen was in the kitchen eating bread and honey;
The maid was in the garden hanging out the clothes,
There came a little blackbird and nipped off her nose.

To market, to market, to buy a fat pig,
Home again, home again, jiggety, jig.

Ride a cock horse
To Banbury Cross
To see what Tommy can buy:
A penny white loaf,
A penny white cake,
And a two-penny apple pie.

Little Tee Wee,
He went to sea
In an open boat;
And while afloat
The little boat bended,
And my story's ended.

Intery, mintery, cutery-corn,
Apple seed and apple thorn;
Wire, brier, limber-lock,
Five geese in a flock,
Sit and sing by a spring,
O-u-t, and in again.

Who made the pie?
I did.
Who stole the pie?
He did.
Who found the pie?
She did.
Who ate the pie?
You did.
Who cried for pie?
We all did.

Elizabeth, Elspeth, Betsy and Bess,
They all went together to seek a
    bird's nest;
They found a bird's nest with five
    eggs in it,
They all took one and left four
    in it.

Little girl, little girl, where have
    you been?
Gathering roses to give to the
    queen.
Little girl, little girl, what gave
    she you?
She gave me a diamond as big as
    my shoe.

Jerry Hall, he was so small,
A rat could eat him, hat and all.

There was a man of double deed,
Sowed his garden full of seed.
When the seed began to grow,
'Twas like a garden full of snow;

When the snow began to melt,
'Twas like a ship without a belt;
When the ship began to sail,
'Twas like a bird without a tail;

When the bird began to fly,
'Twas like an eagle in the sky;
When the sky began to roar,
'Twas like a lion at the door;

When the door began to crack,
'Twas like a stick across my back;
When my back began to smart,
'Twas like a penknife in my heart;
When my heart began to bleed,
'Twas death and death and
    death indeed.

Little Miss Muffet
Sat on a tuffet,
Eating some curds and whey;
There came a great spider,
And sat down beside her,
And frightened Miss Muffet away.

Three wise men of Gotham
Went to sea in a bowl,
And if the bowl had been stronger
My song had been longer.

There were two birds sat upon a stone,
   Fal de ral—al de ral—laddy.
One flew away and then there was one,
   Fal de ral—al de ral—laddy.
The other flew after and then there was none,
   Fal de ral—al de ral—laddy.
So the poor stone was left all alone,
   Fal de ral—al de ral—laddy.
One of these little birds back again flew,
   Fal de ral—al de ral—laddy.
The other came after and then there were two,
   Fal de ral—al de ral—laddy.
Says one to the other: "Pray, how do you do?"
   Fal de ral—al de ral—laddy.
"Very well, thank you, and pray how are you?"
   Fal de ral—al de ral—laddy.

This is the house that Jack built.
This is the malt
That lay in the house that Jack
built.
This is the rat,
That ate the malt
That lay in the house that Jack
built.
This is the cat,
That killed the rat,
That ate the malt
That lay in the house that Jack
built.
This is the dog,
That worried the cat,
That killed the rat,
That ate the malt
That lay in the house that Jack
built.

This is the cow with the crumpled
horn,
That tossed the dog,
That worried the cat,
That killed the rat,
That ate the malt
That lay in the house that Jack
built.
This is the maiden all forlorn,
That milked the cow with the
crumpled horn,
That tossed the dog,
That worried the cat,
That killed the rat,
That ate the malt
That lay in the house that Jack
built.
This is the man all tattered and
torn,
That kissed the maiden all forlorn,
That milked the cow with the
crumpled horn,
That tossed the dog,
That worried the cat,
That killed the rat,
That ate the malt
That lay in the house that Jack
built.

This is the priest all shaven and
    shorn,
That married the man all tattered
    and torn,
That kissed the maiden all forlorn
That milked the cow with the
    crumpled horn,
That tossed the dog,
That worried the cat,
That killed the rat,
That ate the malt
That lay in the house that Jack
    built.
This is the cock that crowed in
    the morn,
That waked the priest all shaven
    and shorn,
That married the man all tattered
    and torn,
That kissed the maiden all forlorn
That milked the cow with the
    crumpled horn,
That tossed the dog,
That worried the cat,
That killed the rat,
That ate the malt
That lay in the house that Jack
    built.

This is the farmer sowing the corn,
That kept the cock that crowed in
    the morn.
That waked the priest all shaven
    and shorn,
That married the man all tattered
    and torn,
That kissed the maiden all forlorn,
That milked the cow with the
    crumpled horn,
That tossed the dog,
That worried the cat,
That killed the rat,
That ate the malt
That lay in the house that Jack
    built.

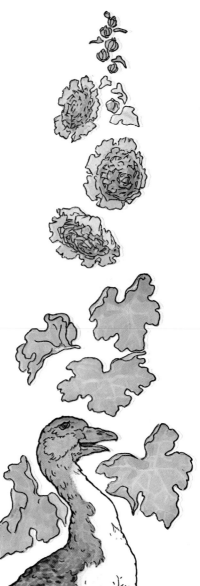

Bye, Baby bunting,
Father's gone a-hunting,
Mother's gone a-milking,
Sister's gone a-silking,
And Brother's gone to buy a skin
To wrap the Baby bunting in.

Little Polly Flinders
Sat among the cinders
    Warming her pretty little toes;
Her mother came and caught her,
Whipped her little daughter
    For spoiling her nice new clothes.

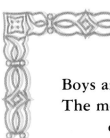

Boys and girls come out to play,
The moon doth shine as bright as
    day,
Leave your supper and leave your
    sleep,
And meet your playfellows in the
    street;
Come with a whoop and come with
    a call,
And come with a good will, or not
    at all.
Up the ladder and down the wall,
A halfpenny roll will serve us all.
You find milk and I'll find flour,
And we'll have a pudding in half
    an hour.

There was a little man,
And he had a little gun,
And his bullets were made of lead,
    lead, lead;
He went to the brook,
And saw a little duck,
And shot it through the head, head,
    head.

He carried it home
To his good wife Joan,
And bade her a fire to make, make,
    make;
To roast the little duck
He had shot in the brook,
And he'd go fetch the drake, drake,
    drake.

A was an Apple pie;
  B bit it;
    C cut it;
      D dealt it;
        E ate it;
          F fought for it;

G got it;
  H had it;
    I inspected it
    J joined it;
      K kept it;
        L longed for it;
          M mourned for it;

N nodded at it;
  O opened it;
    P peeped in it;
      Q quartered it;
        R ran for it;
          S stole it;

T took it;
  V viewed it;
    W wanted it;
      X, Y, Z, and ampers-and,
        All wished for a piece in
          hand.

Here we go up, up, up,
  And here we go down, down,
    downy,
Here we go backward and forward,
  And here we go round, round,
    roundy.

Tom, Tom, the piper's son,
Stole a pig, and away he run;
    The pig was eat,
    And Tom was beat,
And Tom ran crying down the street.

Jack and Jill went up the hill
  To fetch a pail of water;
Jack fell down and broke his crown,
  And Jill came tumbling after.

London Bridge is broken down,
Dance over my Lady Lee;
London Bridge is broken down,
With a gay lady.

How shall we build it up again?
Dance over my Lady Lee;
How shall we build it up again?
With a gay lady.

Build it up with silver and gold,
Dance over my Lady Lee;
Build it up with silver and gold,
With a gay lady.

Silver and gold will be stole away,
Dance over my Lady Lee;
Silver and gold will be stole away,
With a gay lady.

Build it up with iron and steel,
Dance over my Lady Lee;
Build it up with iron and steel,
With a gay lady.

Iron and steel will bend and bow,
Dance over my Lady Lee;
Iron and steel will bend and bow,
With a gay lady.

Build it up with wood and clay,
Dance over my Lady Lee;
Build it up with wood and clay,
With a gay lady.

Wood and clay will wash away,
Dance over my Lady Lee;
Wood and clay will wash away,
With a gay lady.

Build it up with stone so strong,
Dance over my Lady Lee;
Huzza! 'twill last for ages long,
With a gay lady.

As I was walking in a field of
        wheat,
I picked up something good to
        eat;
Neither fish, flesh, fowl, nor
        bone,
I kept it till it ran alone.

Wine and cakes for gentlemen,
        Hay and corn for horses,
A cup of ale for good old wives,
        And kisses for young lasses.

See, see! What shall I see?
A horse's head where his tail
        should be.

Little fishes in a brook,
Father caught them on a hook,
Mother fried them in a pan,
Johnnie eats them like a man.

Pussy cat, pussy cat, where have you been?
I've been to London to see the Queen.
Pussy cat, pussy cat, what did you there?
I frightened a little mouse under the chair.

Pat a cake, pat a cake, Baker's man;
So I do, master, as fast as I can.
Pat it and prick it and mark it with T,
And then it will serve for Tommy and me.

Little Boy Blue, come blow your horn,
The sheep's in the meadow, the cow's in the corn.
What! Is this the way you mind your sheep,
Under the haycock fast asleep?

There was an old woman tossed in a blanket
　　Seventeen times as high as the moon;
But where she was going no mortal could tell,
　　For under her arm she carried a broom.

"Old woman, old woman, old woman," said I,
"Whither, ah whither, ah whither so high?"
"To sweep the cobwebs from the sky,
　　And I'll be with you by and by."

My dear, do you know
How, a long time ago,
    Two poor little children,
Whose names I don't know,

Were stolen away
On a fine summer's day,
    And left in a wood,
As I've heard people say?

And when it was night,
So sad was their plight,
    The sun it went down,
And the moon gave no light!

They sobbed and they sighed,
And they bitterly cried,
    And the poor little things
They laid down and died.

And when they were dead,
The robins so red
    Brought strawberry leaves
And over them spread.

And all the day long
They sang them this song:
"Poor babes in the wood!
Poor babes in the wood!
    And don't you remember
The babes in the wood?"

A hill full, a hole full,
Yet you cannot catch a bowl full.

Rock-a-bye baby,
Thy cradle is green;
Father's a nobleman,
Mother's a queen,
And Betty's a lady
And wears a gold ring,
And Johnny's a drummer
And drums for the king.

If I'd as much money as I could
    spend,
I never would cry old chairs to
    mend,
Old chairs to mend, old chairs to
    mend;
I never would cry, old chairs to
    mend.
If I'd as much money as I could
    tell,
I never would cry old clothes to
    sell,
Old clothes to sell, old clothes to
    sell;
I never would cry, old clothes to
    sell.

Pussy-cat Mole jumped over a coal,
And in her best petticoat burnt a
    great hole.
Poor pussy's weeping, she'll have
    no more milk
Until her best petticoat's mended
    with silk.

Cold and raw the north winds blow
Bleak in the morning early,
All the hills are covered with snow,
And winter's now come fairly.

The man in the moon came down too soon
    To inquire the way to Norridge;
The man in the south, he burnt his mouth
    With eating cold plum porridge.

Four-and-twenty tailors
    Went to kill a snail;
The best man among them
    Durst not touch her tail;
She put out her horns
    Like a little Kyloe cow.
Run, tailors, run, or
    She'll kill you all just now.

Lucy Locket lost her pocket,
Kitty Fisher found it;
There was not a penny in it,
But a ribbon round it.

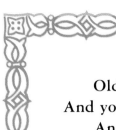

Old Sir Simon the king,
And young Sir Simon the squire,
And old Mrs. Hickabout
Kicked Mrs. Kickabout
Round about our coal fire.

Round and round the rugged rock
The ragged rascal ran.
How many R's are there in that?
Now tell me if you can.

Bessy Bell and Mary Gray,
They were two bonny lasses;
They built their house upon the lea,
And covered it with rushes.

Bessy kept the garden gate,
And Mary kept the pantry;
Bessy always had to wait,
While Mary lived in plenty.

Swan, swan, over the sea;
Swim, swan, swim!
Swan, swan, back again;
Well swum, swan!

There is a well
As round as an apple, as deep as a
cup,
And all the king's horses can't fill
it up.

As little Jenny Wren
Was sitting by her shed.
She waggled with her tail,
And nodded with her head.

She waggled with her tail,
And nodded with her head,
As little Jenny Wren
Was sitting by the shed.

There was a little boy and a
little girl
Lived in an alley;
Says the little boy to the little
girl,
"Shall I, oh, shall I?"

Says the little girl to the little
boy,
"What shall we do?"
Says the little boy to the little
girl,
"I will kiss you."

The boughs do shake and the bells
do ring,
So merrily comes our harvest in,
Our harvest in, our harvest in,
So merrily comes our harvest in.

We've ploughed, we've sowed,
We've reaped, we-ve mowed,
We've got our harvest in.

Little Tom Tucker
Sings for his supper.
What shall he eat?
White bread and butter.
How will he cut it
Without e'er a knife?
How will he marry
Without e'er a wife?

"To bed, to bed," says Sleepy-Head;
"Let's stay awhile," says Slow;
"Put on the pot," says Greedy-Sot,
"We'll sup before we go."

Diddle, diddle, dumpling, my son John,
Went to bed with his breeches on,
One stocking off, and one stocking on,
Diddle, diddle, dumpling, my son John.

High diddle diddle,
The cat and the fiddle,
The cow jumped over the moon;
The little dog laughed
To see such craft,
And the dish ran away with the spoon.

If you sneeze on Monday, you
    sneeze for danger;
Sneeze on a Tuesday, kiss a
    stranger;
Sneeze on a Wednesday, sneeze for
    a letter;
Sneeze on a Thursday, something
    better.
Sneeze on a Friday, sneeze for
    sorrow;
Sneeze on a Saturday, joy
    tomorrow.

Margaret wrote a letter,
Sealed it with her finger,
Threw it in the dam
For the dusty miller.
Dusty was his coat,
Dusty was the silver,
Dusty was the kiss
I'd from the dusty miller
If I had my pockets
Full of gold and silver,
I would give it all
To my dusty miller.

Clap, clap handies,
Mammie's wee, wee ain;
Clap, clap handies,
Daddie's comin' hame;
Hame till his bonny wee bit laddie:
Clap, clap handies,
My wee, wee ain.

Dance to your daddie,
    My bonnie laddie,
Dance to your daddie, my bonnie
    lamb!
You shall get a fishie,
    On a little dishie,
You shall get a fishie when the
    boat comes home.

Dance to your daddie,
    My bonnie laddie,
Dance to your daddie, and to your
    mammie sing!
You shall get a coatie,
    And a pair of breekies,
You shall get a coatie when the
    boat comes in.

Cocks crow in the morn
    To tell us to rise,
And he who lies late
    Will never be wis
For early to bed
    And early to rise
Is the way to be healthy,
    Wealthy and wise.

Oh where, oh where has my little
    dog gone?
Oh where, oh where can he be?
With his ears cut short and his
    tail cut long,
Oh where, oh where is he?

The two gray kits,
And the gray kits' mother,
All went over
The bridge together.

The bridge broke down,
They all fell in;
"May the rats go with you,"
Says Tom Bolin.

Robin and Richard
     Were two pretty men;
They stayed in bed
     Till the clock struck ten.
Then up starts Robin
     And looks at the sky:
"Oh, brother Richard,
     The sun's very high.
You go before
     With the bottle and bag,
And I will come after
     On little Jack nag."

Anna Maria she sat on the fire;
The fire was too hot, she sat on
　　the pot;
The pot was too round, she sat on
　　the gound;
The ground was too flat, she sat
　　on the cat;
The cat ran away with Maria on
　　her back.

Cobbler, cobbler mend my shoe
Get it done by half past two;
Stitch it up, and stitch it down,
Then I'll give you half a crown.

Thirty days hath September,
April, June, and November;
February has twenty-eight alone,
All the rest have thirty—one,
Excepting leap-year, that's the
　　time
When February's days are twenty-
　　nine.

The cock's on the housetop
　　blowing his horn;
The bull's in the barn a-threshing
　　of corn;
The maids in the meadows are
　　making of hay;
The ducks in the river are
　　swimming away.

Ladies and gentlemen come to
　　supper—
Hot boiled beans and very good
　　butter.

Christmas is coming, the geese are
　　getting fat,
Please to put a penny in an old
　　man's hat;
If you haven't got a penny a
　　ha'penny will do,
If you haven't got a ha'penny,
　　God bless you.

John Bull, John Bull,
Your belly's so full,
You can't jump over
A three-legged stool.

As I walked by myself,
And talked to myself,
Myself said unto me:
"Look to thyself,
Take care of thyself,
For nobody cares for thee."

I answered myself,
And said to myself
In the self—same repartee:
"Look to thyself,
Or not look to thyself,
The self—same thing will be."

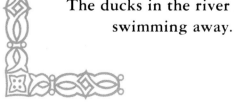

Is John Smith within?—Yes, that he is.
Can he set a shoe?   Ay, marry, two.
Here a nail and there a nail,
Tick—tack—too.

I had a little hen, the prettiest ever seen,
She washed me the dishes and kept the house clean.
She went to the mill to fetch me some flour,
And always got home in less than an hour.
She baked me my bread, she brewed me my ale,
She sat by the fire and told many a fine tale.

When I was a little boy I lived by myself,
And all the bread and cheese I got I put upon a shelf;
The rats and the mice, they made such a strife,
I was forced to go to London to buy me a wife.
The streets were so broad and the lanes were so narrow,
I was forced to bring my wife home in a wheelbarrow;
The wheelbarrow broke and my wife had a fall,
And down came the wheelbarrow, wife and all.

'Twas once upon a time, when Jenny Wren was young,
So daintily she danced and so prettily she sung,
Robin Redbreast lost his heart, for he was a gallant bird,
So he doffed his hat to Jenny Wren, requesting to be heard.

"O, dearest Jenny Wren, if you will but be mine,
You shall feed on cherry pie and drink new currant wine,
I'll dress you like a goldfinch or any peacock gay,
So, dearest Jen, if you'll be mine let us appoint the day."

Jenny blushed behind her fan and thus declared her mind:
"Since, dearest Bob, I love you well, I take your offer kind;
Cherry pie is very nice and so is currant wine,
But I must wear my plain brown gown and never go too fine."

How many days has my baby to play?
  Saturday, Sunday, Monday,
  Tuesday, Wednesday, Thursday, Friday,
  Saturday, Sunday, Monday.

Humpty Dumpty sat on a wall,
Humpty Dumpty had a great fall;
All the king's horses and all the king's men
Couldn't put Humpty Dumpty together again.

Three blind mice! See how they
run!
They all ran after the farmer's
wife,
Who cut off their tails with a
carving knife.
Did you ever see such a thing in
your life
As three blind mice?

Sleep, baby, sleep,
Our cottage value is deep:
The little lamb is on the green,
With woolly fleece so soft and
clean —
Sleep, baby, sleep.

Sleep, baby, sleep,
Down where the woodbines creep;
Be always like the lamb so mild,
A kind, and sweet, and gentle
child.
Sleep, baby, sleep.

One, he loves; two, he loves;
Three, he loves, they say;
Four, he loves with all his heart;
Five, he casts away.
Six, he loves; seven, she loves;
Eight, they both love.
Nine, he comes; ten, tarries;
Eleven, he courts; twelve, he
marries.

Here sits the Lord Mayor,
Here sits his two men,
Here sits the cock,
Here sits the hen,
Here sits the little chickens,
Here they run in,
Chin chopper, chin chopper,
Chin chopper, chin!

As I was going to sell my eggs
I met a man with bandy legs,
Bandy legs and crooked toes;
I tripped up his heels,
And he fell on his nose.

March winds and April showers
Bring forth May flowers.

I see the moon,
And the moon sees me;
God bless the moon,
And God bless me.

Nose, nose,
Jolly red nose,
And what gave thee
That jolly red nose?
Nutmeg and ginger,
Cinnamon and cloves,
That's what gave me
This jolly red nose.

Little King Boggen he built a fine hall,
Pie-crust and pastry-crust, that was the wall;
The windows were made of black puddings and white,
And slated with pancakes,—you ne'er saw the like!

As I went to Bonner
    I met a pig
    Without a wig,
Upon my word and honor.

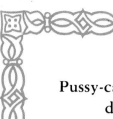

Pussy-cat ate the dumplings, the
    dumplings,
Pussy-cat ate the dumplings.
Mamma stood by, and cried, "Oh,
    fie!
Why did you eat the dumplings?"

There was a little woman, as I've
    been told,
Who was not very young, nor yet
    very old;
Now this little woman her living
    got
By selling codlins, hot, hot, hot!

Dickery, dickery, dare,
The pig flew up in the air;
The man in brown soon brought
    him down,
Dickery, dickery, dare.

You shall have an apple,
You shall have a plum,
You shall have a rattle,
When papa comes home.

Donkey, donkey, old and gray,
Open your mouth and gently bray;
Lift your ears and blow your horn,
To wake the world this sleepy
    morn.

Hannah Bantry,
In the pantry,
Gnawing at a mutton bone;
How she gnawed it,
How she clawed it,
When she found herself alone.

If you are to be a gentleman,
And I suppose you'll be,
You'll neither laugh nor smile,
For a tickling of the knee.

Ring-a-ring-a-roses,
A pocket full of posies;
Hush! hush! hush! hush!
We're all tumbled down.

One, Two—buckle my shoe;
Three, Four—open the door;
Five, Six—pick up sticks;
Seven, Eight—lay them straight;
Nine, Ten—a good fat hen;
Eleven, Twelve—I hope you're
    well;
Thirteen, Fourteen—draw the
    curtain;
Fifteen, Sixteen—the maid's in the
    kitchen;
Seventeen, Eighteen—she's in
    waiting;
Nineteen, Twenty—my stomach's
    empty.

Little Jack Horner
Sat in a corner
Eating a Christmas pie;
He put in his thumb,
And pulled out a plum,
And said: "Oh, what a good boy am I!"

Miss Jane had a bag and a mouse was in it;
She opened the bag, he was out in a minute.
The cat saw him jump and run under the table,
And the dog said: "Catch him, Puss, soon as you're able."

The Queen of Hearts,
She made some tarts
All on a summer's day;
The Knave of Hearts,
He stole those tarts,
And took them clean away.

The King of Hearts
Called for the tarts,
And beat the Knave full sore;
The Knave of Hearts
Brought back the tarts,
And vowed he'd steal no more.

Goosey, goosey, gander, where dost thou wander?
Upstairs and downstairs and in my lady's chamber;
There I met an old man that wouldn't say his prayers,
I took him by his hind legs and threw him downstairs.

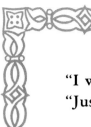

"I went up one pair of stairs."
"Just like me."

"I went up two pairs of stairs."
"Just like me."

"I went into a room."
"Just like me."

"I looked out of a window."
"Just like me."

"And there I saw a monkey."
"Just like me."

Mary had a pretty bird,
Feathers bright and yellow,
Slender legs—upon my word
He was a pretty fellow!

The sweetest note he always sung,
Which much delighted Mary.
She often, where the cage was
        hung,
Sat hearing her canary.

As I went through the garden gap,
Who should I meet but Dick
        Redcap!
A stick in his hand, a stone in
        his throat,
If you'll tell me this riddle,
I'll give you a groat.

St. Dunstan, as the story goes,
Once pulled the devil by his nose,
With red hot tongs, which made
        him roar,
That could be heard ten miles or
        more.

Terence McDiddler,
    The three-stringed fiddler,
Can charm, if you please,
    The fish from the seas.

A duck and a drake,
And a halfpenny cake,
With a penny to pay the old baker.
A hop and a scotch
Is another notch,
Slitherum, slatherum, take her.

Punch and Judy
Fought for a pie;
Punch gave Judy
A knock in the eye.
Says Punch to Judy,
Will you have any more?
Says Judy to Punch,
My eye is too sore.

Cry, baby, cry,
Put your finger in your eye,
And tell your mother it wasn't I.

See saw, Margery Daw,
   Jacky shall have a new master:
Jacky must have but a penny a day
Because he can work no faster.

Daffy-down-dilly is now come to town
With a petticoat green and a bright yellow gown.

"Cock, cock, cock, cock,
    I've laid an egg,
    Am I to gang ba-are-foot?"

"Hen, hen, hen, hen,
    I've been up and down
    To every shop in town,
    And cannot find a shoe
    To fit your foot,
    If I'd crow my hea-art out."

The lion and the unicorn
    Were fighting for the crown.
The lion beat the unicorn
    All about the town.
Some gave them white bread,
    And some gave them brown;
Some gave them plum-cake,
    And sent them out of town.

A frog he would a-wooing go,
  Heigh ho! says Rowley,
Whether his mother would let
  him or no.
  With a rowley, powley,
    gammon and spinach,
  Heigh ho! says Anthony
  Rowley.

So off he set with his opera hat,
  Heigh ho! says Rowley,
And on the road he met with
  a rat.
  With a rowley, powley,
    gammon and spinach,
  Heigh ho! says Anthony
  Rowley.

Pray, Mister Rat, will you go
  with me?
  Heigh ho! says Rowley,
Kind Mistress Mousey for to
  see?
  With a rowley, powley,
    gammon and spinach,
  Heigh ho! says Anthony
  Rowley.

They came to the door of
  Mousey's hall,
  Heigh ho! says Rowley,
They gave a loud knock, and
  they gave a loud call.
  With a rowley, powley,
    gammon and spinach,
  Heigh ho! says Anthony
  Rowley.

Pray, Mistress Mouse, are you
  within?
  Heigh ho! says Rowley,
Oh yes, kind sirs, I'm sitting
  to spin.
  With a rowley, powley,
    gammon and spinach,
  Heigh ho! says Anthony
  Rowley.

Pray, Mistress Mouse, will you
  give us some beer?
  Heigh ho! says Rowley,
For Froggy and I are fond of
  good cheer.
  With a rowley, powley,
    gammon and spinach,
  Heigh ho! says Anthony
  Rowley.

As I was going to Derby
    Upon a market day,
I met the finest ram, sir,
    That ever was fed on hay.

This ram was fat behind, sir,
    This ram was fat before,
This ram was three yards high,
    sir,
    Indeed he was no more.

The wool upon his back, sir,
    Reached up unto the sky,
The eagles built their nests
    there,
    For I heard the young ones
    cry.

The wool upon his tail, sir,
    Was three yards and an ell,
Of it they made a rope, sir,
    To pull the parish bell.

The space between the horns,
    sir,
    Was as far as man could
    reach,
And there they built a pulpit,
    But no one in it preached.

This ram had four legs to walk
    upon,
    This ram had four legs to
    stand,
And every leg he had, sir,
    Stood on an acre of land.

Now the man that fed the ram,
    sir,
    He fed him twice a day,
And each time that he fed him,
    sir,
    He ate a rick of hay.

The man that killed the ram, sir,
    Was up to his knees in
    blood,
And the boy that held the pail,
    sir,
    Was carried away in the
    flood.

Indeed, sir, it's the truth, sir,
    For I never was taught to
    lie,
And if you go to Derby, sir,
    You may eat a bit of the
    pie.

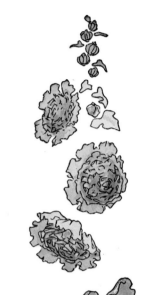

Old King Cole
Was a merry old soul,
And a merry old soul was he;
He called for his pipe,
And he called for his bowl,
And he called for his fiddlers three.

Mistress Mary, quite contrary,
How does your garden grow?
With silver bells and cockle shells
And pretty maids all in a row.

I went to the toad that lies under
    the wall,
I charmed him out, and he came at
    my call;
I scratched out the eyes of the owl
    before,
I tore the bat's wing; what would
    you have more?

See a pin and pick it up,
All the day you'll have good luck.
See a pin and let it lay,
Bad luck you'll have all the day.

Hot-cross buns!
Hot-cross buns!
One a penny, two a penny,
Hot-cross buns!

If ye have no daughters,
Give them to your sons.
One a penny, two a penny,
Hot-cross buns!

Oh, I am so happy!
    A little girl said,
As she sprang like a lark
    From her low trundle bed.
It is morning, bright morning,
    Good morning, papa!
Oh, give me one kiss
    For good morning, mamma!

Diddlty, diddlty, dumpty,
The cat ran up the plum tree;
Give her a plum and down she'll
    come,
Diddlty, diddlty, dumpty.

As Tommy Snooks and Bessie
    Brooks
Were walking out one Sunday;
Says Tommy Snooks to Bessie
    Brooks,
"To-morrow—will be Monday."

Ride a cock horse to Shrewsbury
    Cross,
To buy little Johnny a galloping
    horse.
It trots behind and it ambles
    before
And Johnny shall ride till he can
    ride no more.

Now I lay me down to sleep,
I pray the Lord my soul to keep;
And if I die before I wake,
I pray the Lord my soul to take.

If wishes were horses,
    Beggers might ride;
If turnips were watches,
    I would wear one by my side.

Bonny lass, pretty lass,
   Wilt thou be mine?
Thou shalt not wash dishes
   Nor yet serve the swine.
Thou shalt sit on a cushion
   And sew a fine seam,
And thou shalt eat strawberries,
   Sugar and cream.

Handy-spandy, Jacky dandy,
Loves plum cake and sugar candy.
He bought some at a grocer's shop,
And pleased away went hop, hop, hop.

Ding–dong–bell, the cat's in the well.
  Who put her in?   Little Johnny Green.
  Who pulled her out?   Great Johnny Stout.
    What a naughty boy was that
    To drown poor pussy cat
  Who never did him any harm,
  And killed the mice in his father's barn.

This pig went to market,
That pig stayed at home;
This pig had roast meat,
That pig had none;
This pig went to the barn door,
And cried "week, week," for more.

Come when you're called,
Do what you're bid,
Shut the door after you,
Never be chid.

A was an archer,
    who shot at a frog;
B was a butcher,
    and had a great dog.
C was a captain,
    all covered with lace;
D was a drunkard,
    and had a red face.
E was an esquire,
    with pride on his brow;
F was a farmer,
    and followed the plough.
G was a gamester,
    who had but ill-luck;
H was a hunter,
    and hunted a buck.
I was an innkeeper,
    who loved to carouse;
J was a joiner,
    and built up a house.
K was King William,
    once governed this land;
L was a lady,
    who had a white hand.
M was a miser,
    and hoarded up gold;
N was a nobleman,
    gallant and bold.

O was an oyster girl,
    and went about town;
P was a parson,
    and wore a black gown.
Q was a queen,
    who wore a silk slip;
R was a robber,
    and wanted a whip.
S was a sailor,
    and spent all he got;
T was a tinker,
    and mended a pot.
U was a usurer,
    a miserable elf;
V was a vintner,
    who drank all himself.
W was a watchman,
    and guarded the door;
X was expensive,
    and so became poor.
Y was a youth,
    that did not love school;
Z was a zany,
    a poor harmless fool.

Blind man, blind man,
    Sure you can't see?
Turn round three times,
    And try to catch me.
Turn east, turn west,
    Catch as you can,
Did you think you'd caught me?
    Blind, blind man!

There were two blackbirds sitting on a hill,
One named Jack and the other named Jill.
Fly away, Jack!   Fly away, Jill!
Come again, Jack!   Come again, Jill!

Cross patch, draw the latch,
    Sit by the fire and spin;
Take a cup and drink it up,
    Then call your neighbors in.

Old Mother Hubbard
Went to the cupboard
    To get her poor dog a bone;
But when she came there
The cupboard was bare,
    And so the poor dog had none.

Pease-porridge hot,
  Pease-porridge cold,
Pease-porridge in the pot
  Nine days old.
Spell me that in four letters:
  I will: T H A T.

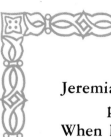

Jeremiah Obadiah, puff, puff,
　　puff.
When he gives his messages he
　　snuffs, snuffs, snuffs,
When he goes to school by day,
　　he roars, roars, roars,
When he goes to bed at night
　　he snores, snores, snores,
When he goes to Christmas treat
　　he eats plum-duff,
Jeremiah Obadiah, puff, puff,
　　puff.

Down by the river
　　Where the green grass
　　grows
Pretty Polly Perkins
　　Bleaches her clothes.
She laughs and she sings,
　　And she sings so sweet.
She calls, Come over,
　　Across the street.
He kissed her, he kissed her,
　　He took her to town;
He bought her a ring
　　And a damascene gown.

Christmas comes but once a year,
And when it comes it brings
　　good cheer,
A pocket full of money, and a
　　cellar full of beer.

A swarm of bees in May
Is worth a load of hay;
A swarm of bees in June
Is worth a silver spoon;
A swarm of bees in July
Is not worth a fly.

Betty Botter bought some butter,
But she said, the butter's bitter;
If I put it in my batter
It will make my batter bitter,
But a bit of better butter,
That would make my batter
　　better.
So she bought a bit of butter
Better than her bitter butter,
And she put it in her batter
And the batter was not bitter.
So t'was better Betty Botter
Bought a bit of better butter.

Mrs Mason bought a basin,
Mrs Tyson said, What a nice
　　'un,
What did it cost? said
　　Mrs Frost,
Half a crown, said Mrs Brown,
Did it indeed, said Mrs Reed,
It did for certain, said Mrs
　　Burton.
Then Mrs Nix up to her tricks
Threw the basin on the bricks.

Polly, put the kettle on,
Polly, put the kettle on,
Polly, put the kettle on,
 We'll all have tea.
Sukey, take it off again,
Sukey, take it off again,
Sukey, take it off again,
 They're all gone away.

The sow came in with the saddle,
The little pig rocked the cradle,
The dish jumped up on the table
To see the pot swallow the ladle.
The spit that stood behind the door
Threw the pudding-stick on the floor.
"Odsplut!", said the gridiron,
  "Can't you agree?
I'm the head constable,
  Bring them to me!"

Little Robin Redbreast sat upon a tree,
Up went the Pussy-Cat, and down went he,
Down came Pussy-Cat, away Robin ran;
Says little Robin Redbreast: "Catch me if you can!"

Little Robin Redbreast jumped upon a spade,
Pussy-Cat jumped after him, and then he was afraid.
Little Robin chirped and sang, and what did Pussy say?
Pussy-Cat said: "Mew, mew, mew," and Robin flew away.

Away, birds, away!
Take a little and leave a little,
And do not come again;
For if you do,
I will shoot you through,
And there will be an end to you.

Hey, my kitten, my kitten.
    And hey, my kitten, my deary,
Such a sweet pet as this
    Was neither far nor neary.

For every evil under the sun,
There is a remedy, or there is none.
If there be one, try to find it;
If there be none, never mind it.

Hush-a-bye, baby, lie still with thy
    daddy,
Thy mammy has gone to the mill,
To get some meal to bake a cake,
So pray, my dear baby, lie still.

"Lend me thy mare to ride a mile."
"She is lamed, leaping over a stile."

"Alack! and I must keep the fair!
I'll give thee money for thy mare."

"Oh, Oh! say you so?
Money will make the mare to go!"

The King of France went up the
    hill,
With twenty thousand men;
The King of France came down
    the hill,
And ne'er went up again.

I had two pigeons bright and gay,
They flew from me the other day.
What was the reason they did go?
I cannot tell, for I do not know.

Mother and Father and Uncle Dick
Went to London on a stick;
The stick broke and made a smoke,
And stifled all the London folk.

Oh, my pretty cock, oh, my
    handsome cock,
I pray you, do not crow before
    day,
And your comb shall be made of
    the very beaten gold,
And your wings of the silver so
    gray.

A robin and a robin's son
Once went to town to buy a bun.
They couldn't decide on plum or
    plain,
And so they went back home again.

A farmer went trotting upon his gray mare,
  Bumpety, bumpety, bump,
With his daughter behind him, so rosy and fair,
  Lumpety, lumpety, lump.

A raven cried "Croak," and they all tumbled down,
  Bumpety, bumpety, bump;
The mare broke her knees and the farmer his crown,
  Lumpety, lumpety, lump.

The mischievous raven flew laughing away,
  Bumpety, bumpety, bump,
And vowed he would serve them the same next day,
  Lumpety, lumpety, lump.

There was an old woman
   Sold puddings and pies;
She went to the mill,
   And dust flew in her eyes.
While through the streets,
To all she meets
   She ever cries:
   "Hot Pies—Hot Pies."

"Old woman, old woman, shall we go a-shearing?"
"Speak a little louder, sir, I'm very thick o' hearing."
"Old woman, old woman, shall I kiss you dearly?"
"Thank you, kind sir, I hear very clearly."

My little old man and I fell out;
I'll tell you what 'twas all about:
I had money and he had none,
And that's the way the noise begun.

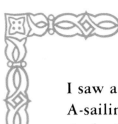

I saw a ship a-sailing,
A-sailing on the sea;
And, oh! it was all laden
With pretty things for thee.

There were comfits in the cabin,
And apples in the hold;
The sails were all of silk,
And the masts were made of gold.

The four-and-twenty sailors
That stood between the decks,
Were four-and-twenty white mice
With chains about their necks.

The captain was a duck,
With a packet on his back;
And when the ship began to move,
The captain said, "Quack! quack!"

Needles and pins, needles and
    pins,
When a man marries his trouble
    begins.

Little boy, little boy, where
    were you born?
Up in the Highlands among the
    green corn.
Little boy, little boy, where did
    you sleep?
In the byre with the kye, in the
    cot with the sheep.

Tommy Trot, a man of law,
Sold his bed and lay upon
    straw;
Sold the straw and slept on
    grass,
To buy his wife a looking-glass.

Magpie, magpie, flutter and flee,
Turn up your tail and good luck
    come to me.

The greedy man is he who sits
And bites out of plates,
Or else takes up an almanac
And gobbles all the dates.

A little cock-sparrow sat on a
    green tree,
And he chirruped, he chirruped,
    so merry was he;
A naughty boy came with his wee
    bow and arrow,
Determined to shoot this little
    cock-sparrow.
"This little cock-sparrow shall
    make me a stew,
And his giblets shall make me a
    little pie, too."
"Oh, no," says the sparrow "I
    won't make a stew."
So he flapped his wings and away
    he flew.

Jack Sprat could eat no fat.
    His wife could eat no lean;
So 'twixt them both they cleared the cloth,
    And licked the platter clean.

There was an old woman, and what do you think?
She lived upon nothing but victuals and drink;
Victuals and drink were the chief of her diet,
And yet this old woman could never be quiet.

What's the news of the day,
Good neighbor, I pray?
They say the balloon
Has gone up to the moon.

There was a crooked man,
     And he went a crooked mile,
He found a crooked sixpence
     Against a crooked stile;
He bought a crooked cat
     Which caught a crooked mouse,
And they all lived together
     In a little crooked house.

Bell horses, bell horses,
    What time of day?
One o'clock, two o'clock,
    Three and away.

One to make ready,
    And two to prepare;
Good luck to the rider,
    And away goes the mare.

One for the money,
    Two for show,
Three to make ready,
    And four to go.

❧⊙☙

Hector Protector was dressed
    all in green;
Hector Protector was sent to
    the Queen.
The Queen did not like him,
No more did the King;
So Hector Pretector was sent
    back again.

❧⊙☙

Of all the gay birds that e'er I
    did see,
The owl is the fairest by far to
    me,
For all day long she sits in a
    tree,
And when the night comes
    away flies she.

Sukey, you shall be my wife
And I will tell you why:
I have got a little pig,
And you have got a sty;
I have got a dun cow,
And you can make good cheese;
Sukey, will you marry me?
Say Yes, if you please.

❧⊙☙

Milkman, milkman, where have
    you been?
In Buttermilk Channel up to my
    chin;
I spilt my milk, and I spoilt my
    clothes,
And got a long icicle hung
    from my nose.

❧⊙☙

The girl in the lane,
That couldn't speak plain,
    Cried, gobble, gobble,
    gobble.
The man on the hill,
That couldn't stand still,
    Went hobble, hobble,
    hobble.

❧⊙☙

Smiling girls, rosy boys,
Come and buy my little toys,
Monkeys made of gingerbread,
And sugar horses painted red.

134

There was a piper had a cow,
  And he had naught to give her;
He pulled out his pipes and played her a tune,
  And bade the cow consider.

The cow considered very well,
  And gave the piper a penny,
And bade him play the other tune,
  "Corn rigs are bonny."

The man in the wilderness
    Asked me
How many strawberries
    Grew in the sea.
I answered him
    As I thought good,
As many red herrings
    As grew in the wood.

Hark! Hark!
The dogs do bark,
The beggars are coming to town;
Some in rags,
Some in tags,
And some in velvet gown.

As I was going to St. Ives
I met seven wives.
Every wife had seven sacks,
Every sack had seven cats,
Every cat had seven kits.
Kits, cats, sacks and wives,
How many were going to St. Ives?

Flour of England, fruit of Spain,
Met together in a shower of
        rain;
Put in a bag, tied round with a
        string;
If you tell me this riddle,
I'll give you a ring.

Up at Piccadilly oh!
    The coachman takes his
        stand,
And when he meets a pretty
        girl,
    He takes her by the hand;
        Whip away forever oh!
        Drive away so clever oh!
        All the way to Bristol oh!
He drives her four-in-hand.

Here's to thee, old apple tree,
Whence thou may'st bud
And whence thou may'st blow,
And whence·thou may'st bear
        apples enow;
Hats full and caps full,
Bushels full and sacks full,
And our pockets full too.

Old Roger is dead and laid in
        his grave,
    Laid in his grave, laid in his
        grave;

Old Roger is dead and laid in
        his grave,
    H'm ha! laid in his grave.

They planted an apple tree
        over his head,
    Over his head, over his
        head;
They planted an apple tree over
        his head,
    H'm ha! over his head.

The apples grew ripe and ready
        to fall,
    Ready to fall, ready to fall;
The apples grew ripe and ready
        to fall,
    H'm ha! ready to fall.

There came an old woman
        a-picking them all,
    A-picking them all,
        a-picking them all;
There came an old woman
        a-picking them all,
    H'm ha! picking them all.

Old Roger jumps up and gives
        her a knock,
    Gives her a knock, gives her
        a knock;
Which makes the old woman go
        hipperty-hop,
    H'm ha! hipperty-hop.

I had a little husband no bigger than my thumb,
I put him in a pint pot, and there I bid him drum;
I bought a little handkerchief to wipe his little nose,
And a pair of little garters to tie his little hose.

Great A, little a,
  Bouncing B;
The cat's in the cupboard,
  And she can't see.

Little Bobby Snooks was fond of
    his books,
And loved by his usher and master;
But naughty Jack Spry, he got a
    black eye,
And carries his nose in a plaster.

Friday night's dream, on Saturday
    told,
Is sure to come true, be it never so
    old.

This is the way the ladies ride,
    Prim, prim, prim.
This is the way the gentlemen ride,
    Trim, trim, trim.
Presently come the country folks.
    Hobbledy gee, hobbledy gee

I saw a fishpond all on fire
I saw a house bow to a squire
I saw a parson twelve feet high
I saw a cottage near the sky
I saw a balloon made of lead
I saw a coffin drop down dead
I saw two sparrows run a race
I saw two horses making lace
I saw a girl just like a cat
I saw a kitten wear a hat
I saw a man who saw these too
And said though strange
    they all were true.

Barber, barber, shave a pig.
How many hairs will make a wig?
Four and twenty; that's enough.
Give the barber a pinch of snuff.

Solomon Grundy,
Born on a Monday,
Christened on Tuesday,
Married on Wednesday,
Took ill on Thursday,
Worse on Friday,
Died on Saturday,
Buried on Sunday.
This is the end
Of Solomon Grundy.

Darby and Joan were dressed in
    black,
Sword and buckle behind their
    back;
Foot for foot, and knee for knee,
Turn about Darby's company.

She sells sea-shells on the sea
    shore;
The shells that she sells are
    sea-shells I'm sure.
So if she sells sea-shells on the
    sea shore,
I'm sure that the shells are
    sea-shore shells.

Bat, bat,
Come under my hat,
And I'll give you a slice of bacon;
And when I bake
I'll give you a cake,
If I am not mistaken.

As I was going up Primrose Hill,
  Primrose Hill was dirty;
There I met a pretty lass,
  And she dropped me a curtsey.

Little lass, pretty lass,
  Blessings light upon you;
If I had half-a-crown a day,
  I'd spend it all upon you.

There was a little boy went into a barn
   And lay down on some hay;
A calf came out and smelled about,
   And the little boy ran away.

When good King Arthur ruled his land
    He was a goodly king;
He stole three pecks of barley meal
    To make a bag-pudding.
A bag-pudding the king did make,
    And stuffed it well with plums,
And in it put great lumps of fat
    As big as my two thumbs.
The king and queen did eat thereof,
    And noblemen beside,
And what they could not eat that night
    The queen next morning fried.

"Jacky, come give me your fiddle,
    If ever you mean to thrive."
"Nay, I'll not give my fiddle
    To any man alive.

"If I should give my fiddle
    They'll think that I'm gone mad,
For many a joyful day
    My fiddle and I have had."

Doctor Foster went to
   Gloucester
In a shower of rain;
He stepped in a puddle,
Right up to his middle,
And never went there again.

There was a mad man he had a
   mad wife,
And they lived in a mad town;
And they had children three at
   birth,
   And mad they were every
   one.
The father was mad, the mother
   was mad,
   And the children mad
   beside;
And they all got on a mad
   horse,
   And madly they did ride.
They rode by night and they
   rode by day,
   Yet never a one of them
   fell;
They rode so madly all the way,
   Till they came to the gates
   of hell.
Old Nick was glad to see them
   so mad,
   And gladly let them in:
But he soon grew sorry to see
   them so merry
And let them out again.

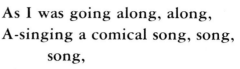

As I was going along, along,
A-singing a comical song, song,
   song,
The lane that I went was so long,
   long, long,
And the song that I sang was so
   long, long, long,
And so I went singing along.

Cackle, cackle, Mother Goose,
Have you any feathers loose?
Truly have I, pretty fellow,
Half enough to fill a pillow.
Here are quills, take one or two,
And down to make a bed for
   you.

In marble walls as white as
   milk,
Lined with a skin as soft as silk,
Within a fountain crystal-clear,
A golden apple doth appear.
No doors there are to this
   stronghold,
Yet thieves break in and steal
   the gold.

Elsie Marley is grown so fine,
She won't get up to feed the
   swine,
But lies in bed till eight or nine.
Lazy Elsie Marley.

One, two, three, four, five,
I caught a hare alive;
Six, seven, eight, nine, ten,
I let him go again.

The north wind doth blow,
And we shall have snow,
And what will poor robin do then?
                    Poor thing!

He'll sit in the barn
And keep himself warm,
And hide his head under his wing.
                    Poor thing!

"You owe me five shillings,"
  Say the bells of St. Helen's.

"When will you pay me?"
  Say the bells of Old Bailey.

"When I grow rich,"
  Say the bells of Shoreditch.

"When will that be?"
  Say the bells of Stepney.

"I do not know,"
  Says the great Bell of Bow.

"Two sticks in an apple,"
  Ring the bells of Whitechapel.

"Halfpence and farthings,"
  Say the bells of St. Martin's.

"Kettles and pans,"
  Say the bells of St. Ann's.

"Brickbats and tiles,"
  Say the bells of St. Giles.

"Old shoes and slippers,"
  Say the bells of St. Peter's.

"Pokers and tongs,"
  Say the bells of St. John's.

It's once I courted as pretty a
    lass,
    As ever your eyes did see;
But now she's come to such a
    pass,
    She never will do for me.
She invited me to her house,
    Where oft I'd been before,
And she tumbled me into the
    hog-tub,
    And I'll never go there any
    more.

For want of a nail
    The shoe was lost,
For want of a shoe
    The horse was lost,
For want of a horse
    The rider was lost,
For want of a rider
    The battle was lost,
For want of a battle
    The kingdom was lost,
And all for the want
    Of a horse shoe nail.

Fee, fi, fo, fum,
I smell the blood of an
    Englishman:
Be he alive or be he dead,
I'll grind his bones to make my
    bread.

Six little mice sat down to spin;
Pussy passed by and she peeped
    in.
What are you doing, my little
    men?
Weaving coats for gentlemen.
Shall I come in and cut off
    your threads?
No, no, Mistress Pussy, you'd
    bite off our heads.
Oh, no, I'll not; I'll help you to
    spin.
That may be so, but you don't
    come in.

Baby and I
    Were baked in a pie,
The gravy was wonderful hot.
    We had nothing to pay
    To the baker that day
And so we crept out of the pot.

Dance, Thumbkin, dance;
    (keep the thumb in motion)
Dance, ye merrymen, everyone.
    (all the fingers in motion)
For Thumbkin, he can dance along.
    (the thumb alone moving)
Thumbkin, he can dance alone.
    (the thumb alone moving)
Dance, Foreman, dance,
    (the first finger moving)
Dance, ye merrymen, everyone.
    (all moving)
But Foreman, he can dance along,
    (the first finger moving)
Foreman, he can dance alone.
    (the first finger moving)
Dance, Longman, dance,
    (the second finger moving)
Dance, ye merrymen, everyone.
    (all moving)
For Longman, he can dance alone,
    (the second finger moving)
Longman, he can dance alone.
    (the second finger moving)
Dance, Ringman, dance,
    (the third finger moving)
Dance, ye merrymen, dance.
    (all moving)
But Ringman cannot dance alone,
    (the third finger moving)

Ringman, he cannot dance alone.
    (the third finger moving)
Dance, Littleman, dance,
    (the fourth finger moving)
Dance, ye merrymen, dance.
    (all moving)
But Littleman, he can dance alone,
    (the fourth finger moving)
Littleman, he can dance alone.
    (the fourth finger moving)

❧❦❧

On Saturday night I lost my
    wife,
And where do you think I
    found her?
Up in the moon, singing a tune,
And all the stars around her.

❧❦❧

Red stockings, blue stockings,
Shoes tied up with silver;
A red rosette upon my breast
And a gold ring on my finger.

153

There was a man in our town,
  And he was wondrous wise,
He jumped into a bramble-bush,
  And scratched out both his eyes;
And when he saw his eyes were out,
  With all his might and main
He jumped into another bush
  And scratched them in again.

INDEX BY FIRST LINE